SHOW · ME · BOOKS

Follow that Car!

A STORY IN RHYME WITH THINGS TO FIND

BY MARCIA LEONARD
PICTURES BY DIANE PALMISCIANO

A BANTAM LITTLE ROOSTER BOOK
TORONTO · NEW YORK · LONDON · SYDNEY · AUCKLAND

For my father
—M.L.

For B.H.W.
—D.P.

FOLLOW THAT CAR!

A Bantam Book / November 1988

Produced by Small Packages, Inc.

"Bantam Little Rooster" is a trademark of Bantam Books.

Library of Congress Cataloging-in-Publication Data

Leonard, Marcia.
  Follow that car!

  (Show me books)
  Summary: A rhyming text follows a car chase through
different kinds of scenery and asks the reader to
point out or find various things in the illustrations.
  [1. Literary recreations.   2. Stories in rhyme]
I. Palmisciano, Diane, ill.   II. Title.   III. Series:
Leonard, Marcia. Show me books.
PZ8.3.L54925Fo 1988   [E]   88-3412
ISBN 0-553-05477-5

Published simultaneously in the United States and Canada

Bantam Books are published by Bantam Books, a division of Bantam
Doubleday Dell Publishing Group, Inc. Its trademark, consisting of the
words "Bantam Books" and the portrayal of a rooster, is Registered in U.S.
Patent and Trademark Office and in other countries. Marca Registrada.
Bantam Books, 666 Fifth Avenue, New York, New York 10103.

PRINTED IN THE UNITED STATES OF AMERICA

RM   0 9 8 7 6 5 4 3 2 1

"Goodbye," said Mr. Pfister, as he hugged his young son Herb.
He hurried to the taxi that was waiting at the curb.
What happened next is legend in the Pfister family—
so read the rhymes that follow and then tell me what you see!

Herb's daddy told the driver, "I am running rather late!
This business trip's important and the airplane will not wait."
"Don't worry," said the driver. "This old car and I won't fail."
Then he took off with a lurch that left Mr. Pfister pale.

What a worn out old car!

Look closely at this picture and please show me if you can,
a skateboard and a wagon and a small delivery van.
Find one door that is open and find four doors that are not.
Then see if you can locate something Herbert's dad forgot.

What else can you show me?

The taxi turned the corner just as Herbie found the case.
"Oh, no!" said Mrs. Pfister, with concern upon her face.
"We'll have to catch your daddy, Herb, so hop into the car."
Then they sped off down the street—but they didn't get too far!

Follow that cab!

Look closely at this picture and find children by the score.
Some are getting on the bus, some are coming out the door.
Three are playing with a ball, two are walking with their bikes.
One is sitting on a bench, talking to a girl he likes.

What else are the kids doing?

The school bus finally drove off, and Herb's mother could move on.
"Oh, dear!" she said. "Can you see where that rattletrap has gone?"
"It's just ahead," said Herbert, "near the center of the town."
So his mom stepped on the gas—but a workman flagged them down.

There goes the car!

Look closely at this picture. What is blocking off the lane?
What is mixing up cement? What is swinging from the crane?
Find a worker with a trowel, who is smoothing out the walk.
Find some men with hard hats on, who just stand around and talk.

What else can you find?

The Pfisters saw the taxi as they left the building site.
(It had crossed the railroad tracks and was waiting for a light.)
But when they reached the crossing they could only sit and sigh,
for the railroad gates were down, and a train was passing by.

Will they ever catch that car?

Look closely at this picture of a train that's hauling freight.
Find a tank car made of steel and a flatcar with a crate.
Find a car that carries logs and some boxcars in a row.
Find the engine at the front that has everything in tow.

What other things can you find?

The gates were finally lifted once the train had rumbled on.
And as Herb had suspected that old taxi cab was gone.
He spied it far ahead, though. (Mrs. Pfister was amazed!)
And they might have caught that car if the bridge had not been raised.

Oh, no! Not another delay!

Look closely at this picture and then point to a canoe,
then a speedy motor boat, then a sailboat with its crew.
Show me someone on the dock, who is fishing with a pole.
Show me someone on the bank, who is going for a stroll.

What else can you point to?

The Pfisters lost the taxi by the time they crossed the bridge.
But then they took a shortcut down a lane along a ridge.
They had to pass a tractor that was moving like a snail.
Still, they made up lots of time and were soon back on the trail.

Follow that car!

Look closely at this picture and then see if you can say
how many geese are swimming and how many cows eat hay.
Count all the baby chickens that are pecking with the hen.
Count all the little piglets that are oinking in the pen.

What else can you count?

The Pfisters reached the airport with just seconds left to spare,
pulling up behind the taxi as Herb's father paid his fare.
"Is something wrong?" he asked them, with confusion on his face.
His wife said, "You forgot this!" and then Herb held out the case.

Hooray! They caught him in time!

Look closely at this picture. Do you see the baggage cart?
And some people in a line, who are waiting to depart?
Now try to find the windsock that is flapping in the breeze,
and an airplane taking off, climbing high above the trees.

What other things do you see?

"Thank you!" cried Mr. Pfister. "You have really saved my life!"
Then he hugged and kissed his son and he kissed and hugged his wife.
His wife said, "Good-bye, darling," and his son said, "So long, Pop!"
Then they got back in the car and drove home without *one* stop.